MR. TICKLE

by Roger Hargreaves

Happy Tickling!
lots of love + filth
on your 22nd
birthday!

Gabbie?
xxx

WORLD INTERNATIONAL

It was a warm, sunny morning.

In his small house at the other side of the wood Mr Tickle was asleep.

You didn't know that there was such a thing as a Tickle, did you?

Well, there is!

Tickles are small and round and they have arms that stretch and stretch and stretch.

Extraordinary long arms!

MORE SPECIAL OFFERS
FOR MR MEN AND LITTLE MISS READERS

In every Mr Men and Little Miss book like this one, and now in the Mr Men sticker and activity books, you will find a special token. Collect six tokens and we will send you a gift of your choice.

Choose either a Mr Men or Little Miss poster, or a Mr Men or Little Miss **double sided** full colour bedroom door hanger.

Return this page with six tokens per gift required to
Marketing Dept., MM / LM Gifts, World International Ltd., Deanway Technology Centre, Wilmslow Road, Handforth, Cheshire SK9 3FB

|— 100 mm —|

Your name:_____ Age: _____

Address: _____

_____

_____Postcode: _____

Parent / Guardian Name (Please Print) _____

Please tape a 20p coin to your request to cover part post and package cost

I enclose six tokens per gift, please send me:- .

Posters:- Mr Men Poster ☐ Little Miss Poster ☐

Door Hangers - Mr Nosey / Muddle ☐ Mr Greedy / Lazy ☐

Mr Tickle / Grumpy ☐ Mr Slow / Quiet ☐

Mr Messy / Noisy ☐

L Miss Fun / Late ☐ L Miss Helpful / Tidy ☐

L Miss Busy / Brainy ☐ L Miss Star / Fun ☐

Please Tick Appropriate Box

ENTRANCE FEE
SAUSAGES

250 mm

MR. GREEDY

Collect six of these tokens
You will find one inside every
Mr Men and Little Miss book
which has this special offer.

1
TOKEN

We may occasionally wish to advise you of other Mr Men gifts.
If you would rather we didn't please tick this box ☐

Offer open to residents of UK, Channel Isles and Ireland o

Mr Men and Little Miss Library Presentation Boxes

In response to the many thousands of requests for the above, we are delighted to advise that these are now available direct from ourselves, for only **£4.99** (inc VAT) plus 50p p & p.
The full colour units accommodate each complete library. They have an integral carrying handle and "push out" bookmark as well as a neat stay closed fastener.
Please do not send cash in the post. Cheques should be made payable to **World International Ltd.** **for the sum of £5.49** (inc p & p) per box.

Return this page with your cheque, stating below which presentation box you would like, **to Mr Men Office, World International Ltd., Deanway Technology Centre, Wilmslow Road, Handforth, Cheshire SK9 3FB.**

Your Name _____

Your Address _____

_____

_____Post Code _____

Name of Parent/Guardian (please print) _____

Signature _____

I enclose a cheque for £ _____ made payable to World International Ltd.

Please send me a Mr Men Presentation Box ☐ (please tick or write in quantity)

Little Miss Presentation Box ☐

Offer applies to UK, Eire & Channel Isles only.

Thank you

Mr Tickle was fast asleep. He was having a dream. It must have been a very funny dream because it made him laugh out loud, and that woke him up.

He sat up in bed, stretched his extraordinary long arms, and yawned an enormous yawn.

Mr Tickle felt hungry, so do you know what he did?

He reached out one of his extraordinary long arms, opened the bedroom door, reached down the stairs, opened the kitchen door, reached into the kitchen cupboard, opened the biscuit tin, took out a biscuit, brought it back upstairs, in through the bedroom door and back to Mr Tickle in bed.

As you can see, it's very useful indeed having arms as long as Mr Tickle's.

Mr Tickle munched his biscuit. He looked out of the window.

"Today looks very much like a tickling day," he thought to himself.

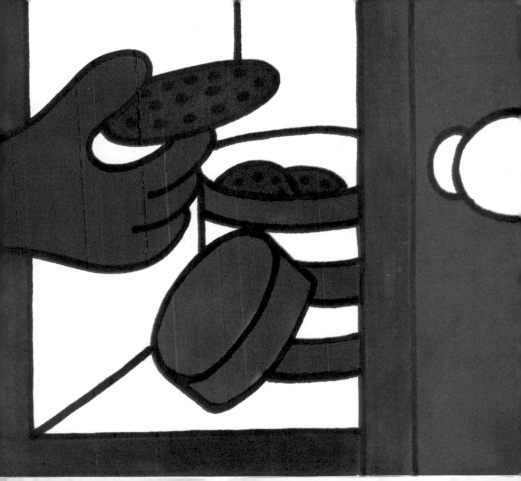

So, later that morning, after Mr Tickle had made his bed and cooked his breakfast, he set off through the wood.

As he walked along, he kept his eyes very wide open, looking for somebody to tickle.

Looking for anybody to tickle!

Eventually Mr Tickle came to a school.

There was nobody about, so, reaching up his extraordinary long arms to a high window ledge, Mr Tickle pulled himself up and peeped in through the open window.

Inside he could see a classroom.

There were children sitting at their desks, and a teacher writing on the blackboard.

Mr Tickle waited a minute and then reached in through the window.

Mr Tickle's extraordinary long arm went right up to the teacher, paused, and then – tickled!

The teacher jumped in the air and turned round very quickly to see who was there.

But there was nobody there!

Mr Tickle grinned a mischievous grin.

He waited another minute, and then tickled the teacher again.

This time he kept on tickling until soon the teacher was laughing out loud and saying, "Stop it! Stop it!" over and over again.

All the children were laughing too at such a funny sight.

There was a terrible pandemonium.

Eventually, Mr Tickle thought that he had had enough fun, so he gave the teacher one more tickle for luck, and then very quietly brought his arm back through the open window.

Chuckling to himself, he jumped down from the window, leaving the poor teacher to explain what it was all about.

Which of course he couldn't.

Then Mr Tickle went to town.

And what a day Mr Tickle had.

He tickled the policeman on traffic duty at the crossroads in the middle of town.

It caused an enormous traffic jam.

He tickled the greengrocer just as he was piling apples neatly in his shop window.

The greengrocer fell over backwards, and the apples rolled all over the shop.

At the railway station, the guard was about to wave his flag for the train to leave.

As he lifted his arm in the air, Mr Tickle tickled him.

And every time he tried to wave his flag, Mr Tickle tickled him until the train was ten minutes late leaving the station and all the passengers were furious.

That day Mr Tickle tickled everybody.

He tickled the doctor.

He tickled the butcher.

He even tickled old Mr Stamp, the postman, who dropped all his letters into a puddle.

Then Mr Tickle went home.

Sitting in his armchair in his small house at the other side of the wood, he laughed and laughed every time he thought about all the people he had tickled.

So, if you are in any way ticklish, beware of Mr Tickle and those extraordinary long arms of his.

Just think. Perhaps he's somewhere about at this very moment while you're reading this book.

Perhaps that extraordinary long arm of his is already creeping up to the door of this room.

Perhaps it's opening the door now and coming into the room.

Perhaps, before you know what is happening, you will be well and truly . . .

. . . tickled!